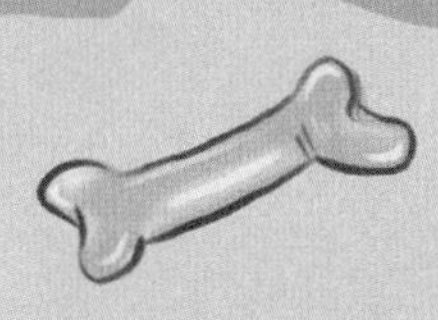

About The Mud Mon

Bullwrinkle and his two best friends, Henry and Hudson, have grown up together playing catch in Hillsdale Park. These young dogs love to play!

On one side of the park is a large area of heavily wooded pine trees, which Bullwrinkle is not allowed to enter by himself.

Hidden in these woods is the legend of The Mud Monster. It lives in deep mud holes. But no one has ever seen it. Who would want to!

When Bullwrinkle decides to enter the woods alone to find a lost ball, he soon discovers whether the rumors of The Mud Monster are real or not.

Bullwrinkle must use his courage and wits to find the lost ball and make it back home safely.

Story Lesson

Each Bullwrinkle & Friends book presents a life lesson for children to learn.

The Mud Monster's Story Lesson

Listening to and following the family rules to keep children safe and out of trouble.

New Words To Learn

Bullwrinkle & Friends books include a new word(s) for your child to learn. *The Mud Monster* includes these new words:

Imagination ***[ih-maj-uh-ney-shuhn]***

A person's ability to form new ideas, images and stories.

Stubborn ***[stub-born]***

When a person refuses to follow rules or goes against good behavior.

Meet Bullwrinkle

Bullwrinkle is a young Shar Pei with an old soul. When Bullwrinkle's curiosity and love for adventure get the best of him, he finds himself in funny situations that teach him valuable lessons. He has a heart of gold and a large funny, expressive and mischievous personality. He's the type of dog that kids would love to have as a friend!

"Great Jelly Donut!"

This is Bullwrinkle's favorite expression when he is surprised or overly excited! "Great Jelly Donut!" expresses his love for the ring-shaped pastry. And it's a fun phrase that is uniquely "Bullwrinkle!"

Other Characters in The Mud Monster

The Mud Monster

Slimy, stinky and scuzzy and always muddy! But is it real or is it a figment of Bullwrinkle's vivid imagination?

Henry

Henry is Bullwrinkle's best friend and the star baseball player at school. He is a strong, athletic black Labrador Retriever who wears a baseball cap.

Hudson

Hudson is Bullwrinkle's other friend. He is nervous, overly cautious, and quick to encourage Bullwrinkle to get into trouble. He's the first to say "I told you so!" Hudson is a goofy golden Newfoundland Retriever.

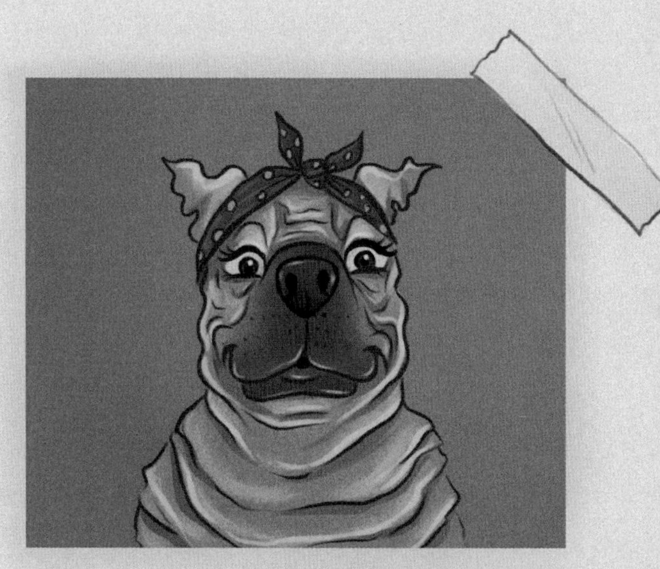

Bullwrinkle's Mom

She is a loving and trusting mom who tries to keep Bullwrinkle in line. Part of her job is to teach Bullwrinkle life lessons to keep him safe and out of trouble. Mom is always right!

BullwrinkleKids.com

Our Mission

to inspire children and parents everywhere with imagination, laughter and a lifetime joy of reading.

Special Thanks to:

The original Bullwrinkle Shar Pei who gave everyone years of joy, laughter and love, and is the inspiration for all Bullwrinkle & Friends books.

Lee Prentiss and Ed Ford who also give everyone their talents, laughter and love.

Published By

irene@bullwrinklekids.com

ISBN 979-8-9888871-0-2

eBook ISDN 979-8-9888871-1-9

Cover & Illustration by Ujala Shahid.

Proudly created and printed in the United States of America.

BULLWRINKLE & FRIENDS

THE MUD MONSTER

CREATED BY

JAY ALLEN & BILL TAYLOR

Bullwrinkle and his two best friends, Henry and Hudson, are playing catch after school in their neighborhood park. Little do they know that Bullwrinkle will soon come face to face with the stinkiest, slimiest, and scuzziest monster...
ThE MUD

MONSTER!
BE AWARE

"This time, Henry, throw it real far toward the woods," yells Bullwrinkle.

Henry is the school baseball star and is very strong. He winds up his arm and throws the ball high, high up into the cool, blue sky.

"I think the ball might get stuck in the clouds," says Hudson. Hudson is overly cautious. Then he gets worried. "Oh no! What if the ball hits the hot sun and burns up?"

Bullwrinkle is running as fast as he can toward the woods looking for the ball, but he doesn't see it.

"Looks like it landed deep in the woods," yells Henry. "But we have to go home and do our homework. Good luck finding the ball!"

"Gee, thanks for nothing, guys," says Bullwrinkle quietly.

Bullwrinkle knows not to go into the woods by himself. It's a family rule. But he says, "What could go wrong?" as he walks in anyway.

His stubborn streak and curiosity usually lead him into trouble!

Bullwrinkle wanders deeper and deeper into the woods looking for the ball.

His mom's voice is in the back of his mind, telling him he should leave and come back tomorrow with Henry and Hudson.

But Bullwrinkle is stubborn and doesn't always listen to his mom.

"I think I'll look over there by those pine trees," he says.

Finally, he spots the ball in the middle of a large, brown mud hole surrounded by tall, green pine trees.

"Oh great, why did the ball have to land in a mud hole," he says. "I hope this mud hole isn't home to one of those nasty Mud Monsters I've heard about."

Rumor has it that The Mud Monster is a stinky, slimy and scuzzy mess of a monster that lives in the bottom of a large mud hole.

But no one has actually seen The Mud Monster. Ever.

“How am I going to get that ball without getting muddy?” he says. “And if I see a Mud Monster, there’s no telling what he’ll do to me.”

First, Bullwrinkle finds a broken branch to try and scoop the ball out of the mud hole. But the branch is too short.

Next, he tries throwing stones into the mud hole so he can walk on them to get the ball. But the stones sink into the mud.

"Why do these tricks work on TV shows, but not for me?" Bullwrinkle wonders.

Finally he decides to tip toe toward the ball quietly and lightly, so he won't sink into the mud.

But the mud is wet, and he slips and sinks deep into the mud hole! The mud is so deep that it goes over his head.

"Great Jelly Donut!" Bullwrinkle yells. It's his favorite expression to shout. "The Mud Monster caught me!"

Bullwrinkle rolls and wrestles in the deep mud hole trying to crawl out. Mud is flying everywhere as he tries to get his footing while fighting The Mud Monster!

"Get away from me, you stinky, slimy and scuzzy Mud Monster!" Bullwrinkle yells. "You will never win against me!"

The struggle continues. Bullwrinkle is holding the ball with one paw and fighting The Mud Monster with the other!

But who's winning? The Mud Monster is stinky, slimy, and scuzzy. And Bullwrinkle is strong, young, and just as stinky now.

He finally escapes out of the mud hole covered in mud dripping from the top of his head to the pads on his paws! The ball is even covered in mud.

“Take that, you dirty old Mud Monster,” says Bullwrinkle. “I won and you lost!”

But the Mud Monster is nowhere in sight.

Was the stinky, slimy, and scuzzy Mud Monster real, or did it come from Bullwrinkle's imagination?

"I'm going to be in so much trouble when I get home," he says. "I'm not allowed to be in these woods by myself. And look how muddy I am."

He begins walking, finds an opening in the woods, and pops out with the muddy ball.

As he walks back home, leaving muddy paw prints along the way, he tries to think of excuses to tell his mom how he got so muddy. He doesn't want to get in trouble.

MONSTER

"I could tell her that the stinky, slimy and scuzzy Mud Monster attacked me in the woods," he says.

"Or I could tell her that I saved a school bus full of children from running into a mud hole."

Bullwrinkle is known to stretch the truth while telling a story.

He has an overactive imagination!

He decides to tell his mom the truth because he knows that honesty is the best policy. Plus, he knows that telling his mom a lie will get him into more trouble!

He'll save The Mud Monster story for another day.

His mom is in the front yard watering the plants when he walks up.

"Young pup are you ok?" asks his mother. "I can't see who you are through all the mud!"

"Mom, it's me, Bullwrinkle, and, um, a muddy ball!"

"What happened? You're covered in mud from head to paw!" says his mom.

"Mom, my friend Henry threw this ball into the woods. I ran in to get it and fell into a deep mud hole," he says.

"I know I'm not allowed to go into the woods alone. I'm sorry that I didn't ask permission."

"Bullwrinkle, our family rules keep you safe and out of trouble," his mother says.

"You're a muddy mess. Let's spray you off with the garden hose!"

Playing in the garden hose is one of Bullwrinkle's favorite things to do!

"Great Jelly Donut!" he shouts with joy.

He celebrates saving the ball and defeating The Mud Monster by doing his special Happy Dance!

"Great Jelly Donut!"

Later that night in the bed, Bullwrinkle thinks about a new adventure for tomorrow. One that doesn't involve mud!

"I can't wait to tell my friends about how I fought that stinky, slimy and scuzzy mess of a Mud Monster," he says.

Do you think The Mud Monster is real or made up by Bullwrinkle's overactive imagination?

Meanwhile back at the mud hole...

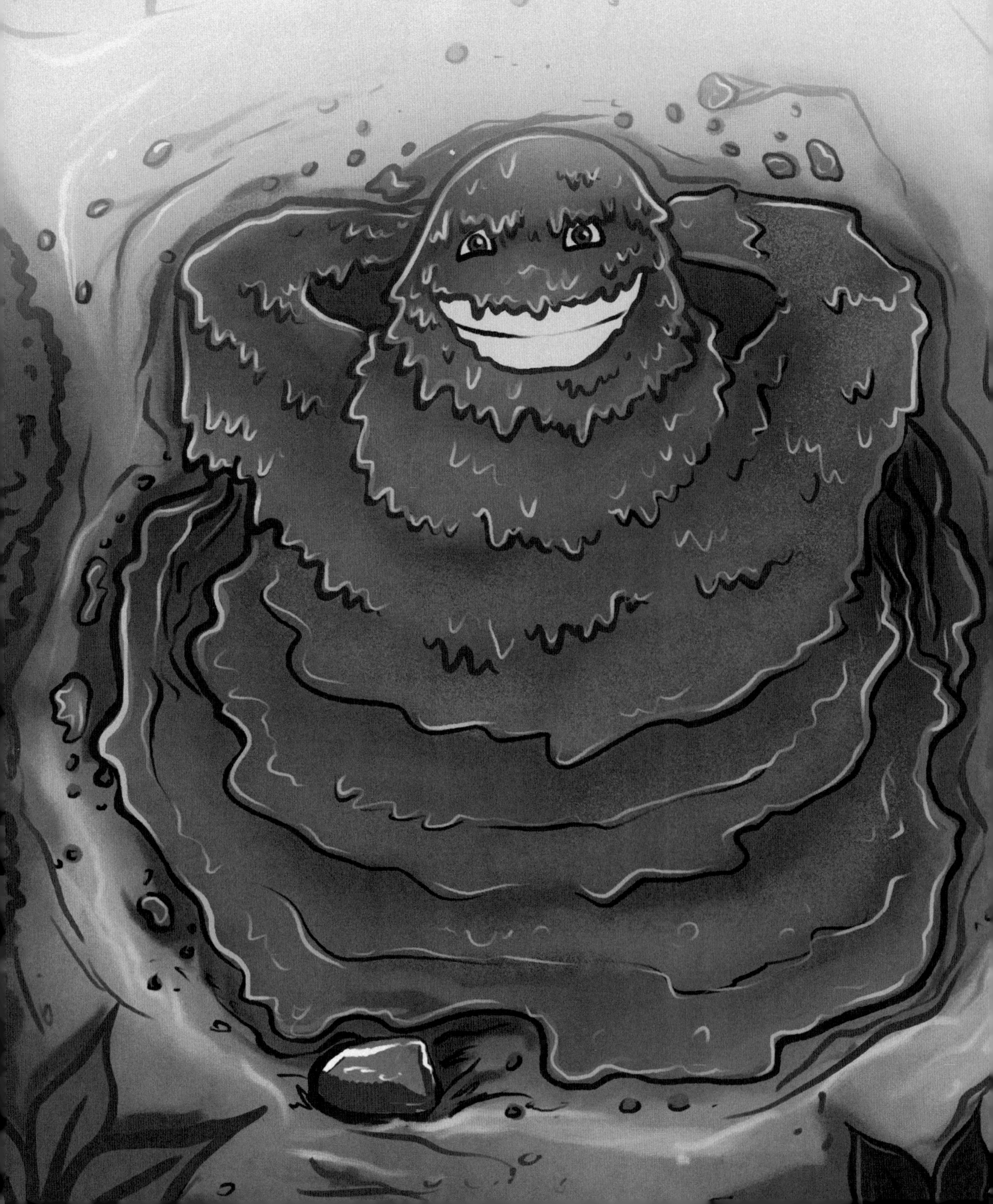

Made in the USA
Las Vegas, NV
31 October 2023